Peninsulas

*stories
by*

KC THORNE

FITHIAN PRESS · SANTA BARBARA · 1997

Published by Fithian Press
A division of Daniel and Daniel, Publishers, Inc.
Post Office Box 1525
Santa Barbara, CA 93102

Book design: Eric Larson

LIBRARY OF CONGRESS CATALOGING-IN-PUBLICATION DATA
Thorne, K.C., (date)
    Peninsulas / by K.C. Thorne.
        p. cm.
    ISBN 1-56474-204-0 (pbk. : alk. paper)
    1. Michigan—Social life and customs—Fiction. I. Title
PS3570.H6555P46   1997
813'.54—dc20   96-27673

For Pam

Your love has given meaning to my life
and inspiration to my words

With gratitude and eternal love

Contents

Peninsulas

A Boy and His Dogs

Although I can no longer recall the first time my old eyes came to rest on the boy, it now seems he's been wandering my beach forever. Though it's by no means possible, there are times I swear that right before dusk I can see him running towards home. Southward he goes with the two dogs, jumping the waves seemingly laughing at their joy. Maybe it was the loneliness of an old man, or just the sight of a relationship developing as theirs was, but until I draw my last breath I'll never forget the drama played out before my eyes.

I had been sitting in this glassed-in porch for more years than the lad had been alive, and with distaste and reluctance I had seen this desolate beach as the city people discovered its unique charm. Solitude seems to have a method of taking what it needs from a soul and leaving only what it chooses. My only entertainment now was watching the boy and his dogs, and painting the lake and sky that I could see from the mechanical chair.

My first memory of him is fuzzy, although I remember him with his mother or possibly a nanny. He was younger then and seemingly sadder, or possibly more withdrawn. Each year I eagerly awaited his early summer arrival on the beach. He grew each winter more than I ever expected, or remembered myself growing as a youth of his age. The sec-

ond or third year, I don't correctly recall, a major change
overcame my unknown friend. He came skipping down the
beach in his customary mid-length shorts and cotton polo
shirt playing his solitary games that he had perfected to his
own desires. I set aside my brushes and oils and rolled to
the window sill to reach the binoculars leaning against the
pane. Focusing the heavy military glasses on him, I inspected my summer companion with the intent of a doctor
doing an annual physical. He had grown, and his nose had
a new crook in it, more than likely the gift of a bully
schoolmate. It took me more than a few minutes to realize
that the change wasn't in my young study, but in the absence of an escort. He was maturing and was now to be
trusted to be alone on the beach without a guardian. I
smiled sadly knowing that in a few more years one of the
true and constant joys of my life would no longer return to
my beach.

Shortly after his arrival that summer another change
happened quite unexpectedly. As he came around the
southern bluff, at his usual full run, two small puppies
came at his heels stumbling from running at a speed too
high for their overgrown paws. Since the death of my own
best friend several years previously I had forgotten how
much I adored the companionship and love of dogs. The
lad's pups were as distinct as two can possibly be. One was
an Irish setter already showing the auburn and red hues
marking his maturity. The other was a German shepherd,
from my viewpoint a female, ears and paws far too large
for her puppyish body. The boy was obviously taking great
delight in showing his new-found friends his secret spot,
on my secluded beach. The pups frolicked and played with
their master, dodging the surf and trying their best to learn
his private games.

That year I spent much time adjusting to a new schedule. I would rise long before dawn to prepare the paints

and brushes for a dawn spell of painting the lake and beach. My wildlife painting had long ago settled my estate, and since the accident I seemed content with painting only my beach and the lake before it. The dawn and dusk were the moments I was trying in vain to capture on canvas. Through the dozens of efforts, none seemed to perfectly capture the grays and reds of the shadows the sunset reflected across the lake. I once thought that maybe only God was a gifted enough artist to capture these special scenes and colors. Each new canvas seemed to be missing something, always looking incomplete, although every year my agent gladly bought them. So each morning I mixed grays and reds, looking for the proper contrast. I painted every morning until he arrived with the pups. When they frolicked onto my beach I set aside the tools and took joy in watching the three of them. With unknown courtesy they went home each day for lunch, allowing me to eat and resume painting. With the consistency of the ore freighters they would come back each day in mid-afternoon to once again resume their games. I watched intently, if not with a touch of envy.

When they left for their supper, I would again resume my mixing of the paints, trying to imitate the colors of the sun as it set over the lake. The beauty of the Great Lakes had captured my soul nearly three quarters of a century before. The changes over my private area of the westerly fresh sea had been invaded in the last twenty years by a host of mechanical water toys, although I could still approve of the sailing vessels and freighters as they plowed their way, making the trade. After dinner they again returned to continue the games that he was teaching his younger friends. Following his evening swim he would settle quietly with a pup on each side and together they would watch as the red sun slowly sank into the lake, with a magical effect that you can only understand from seeing it first hand. As the three of them sat in utter stillness and awe, I would apply oil to canvas with rapid precision.

The routine went on all summer, much to the joy of all four of us. At my age I couldn't identify all the games they played, but some were obvious. Together the two dogs learned to fetch, sit, stay, chase, wrestle and generally have fun. In this their first summer the pups were distinguishable only by the physical differences of their heritage. As the summer shortened and a new school year approached I came to the yearly awareness that my friend's time on my beach was growing short. In the last week the brushes remained still and my study of the youngsters became all-encompassing. The bond that had developed between the three was strong as the rare summer northern gale. During this last week I observed the one small difference between the two dogs. The setter would take part in all the games except the boy's favorite. When it came to wading or playing by the shoreline, he seemed no different from his female companion. When the boy would swim and venture out to the deep clean water the female would follow, but the Irish would only sit completely still very close to the water, watching the others. This reaction seemed strange for many reasons. The dog seemed not to fear the water, nor to dislike being wet. He was just content to play in the shallow water and watch when the boy and German ventured far out into the lake. I dismissed this as a quirk of youth and thought no more of it. I was, in effect, envious of the lad, as each year he had progressed as a swimmer. Now, on the verge of manhood, he had developed into one of the strongest I had ever seen. I remembered the thousands of hours I had spent swimming in the fresh sea with the fondest memories. He loved to venture to the bottom of the lake with snorkel, exploring out of sight of everything but my binoculars.

The summer sadly came to a close on a beautiful

Michigan summer Friday night. They stayed long after sunset that night, watching the planets introduce the multitude of stars and an impressive full moon. The lake shimmered a ghostly silver under the brightness of the night lights and a glimmer of Northern Lights. A tear came to my eye as they walked slowly out of sight around the southern bluff beyond the rocks.

That fall, winter and spring I struggled with the scene I had been trying to capture all summer. Just before Christmas my agent made his annual pilgrimage north and greedily bought all the paintings of red-and-gray lake scenes. I let them go with relief; they taxed my heart in what they didn't say and couldn't show. The seasons passed in a flurry of snow and ice that graced the canvas. By spring I had grown tired of trying to remember the colors of summer. I was still trying, in vain, to paint the difficult images. Eventually I even returned to painting the woodland wildlife that I had made my living by in the early years.

As the summer approached I eagerly anticipated the coming of my friends. My entertainment was trying to imagine any differences or changes of maturity that had occurred. I prayed for their well being and calculated the day of return.

I wasn't prepared for the moment when it finally arrived. When they came around the bluff, I wouldn't have recognized the young man if it hadn't been for the distinctive dogs. My painting for the day ended abruptly as I took the day to marvel at the changes. He had grown towards manhood over the winter, filling out in the legs, arms and shoulders. His hair was dark, as the sun had yet to fade it. He still skipped and bounded with youthful exuberance of returning to his special place. He took all of my attention away from the dogs, my only observation being that they were now nearly fully grown.

I quickly fell back into my summer routine with an uplifting change of attitude. They lifted my spirits immensely, changing the outlook and brightening my world. I guessed that the change in his body was both natural and worked for. He still played with his friends but now spent nearly all his time in the water practicing the different strokes of a competitive swimmer.

Before the Independence Day holiday a major difference in the relationships of the three friends had become apparent to me. Thinking back, it may have been there all summer and only become more obvious as the season progressed. The German shepherd and the boy had become very close and were never more than an arm's length away, in or out of the water. Meanwhile the setter had withdrawn to a friendly but respectable distance. Please don't misunderstand, the friendship between the three was still there, but the Irish seemed content to sit at a distance and watch quietly. When his two friends went far out into the water, he would resume his position, just out of the water's reach looking westward. When they played the games on the beach he would participate, but over the summer he stayed farther and farther away.

As the late summer storms brewed I seemed to find a small piece of the color puzzle. The sky came to shape and parts of the water, but the shadows and reflections on the beach and water weren't quite right. The late summer storms were unusually violent this year and sprinkled the waves with driftwood. I'd never seen so much of the wood, and it provided the three with a new game. The shepherd and the lad would swim all evening, collecting the wood, as their friend patrolled whatever came ashore. The lad would stack the wood far up the beach to dry and would light a fire every Saturday night just before dusk.

As the end of the season approached I came upon the conclusion that the color I longed for would evade me another year. I had resigned myself during the last week to joyfully watching my friends. On that Friday morning I awoke late to an untimely sound. A strong gale had brewed overnight in the north and was sending a cascade of sea and wind sounds ripping through the chateau. The lake was again dotted with driftwood as the waves came crashing around the north bluff, leaving the cove strangely serene. The lad and his friends came late to the beach. He wore an old cap to shield his eyes from the blowing sand, and the dogs' fur blew straight back, thinning their appearance. They resumed the beach games, thankful of the shield from the wind in the cove. The day progressed with the usual annual sadness I had when they left to go south. After dinner I made my drink and settled in to watch the last few hours speed away.

The newest game was the last of the year as they proceeded to pick out the driftwood in the cove. The beach and cove were cleared as I wondered why they bothered, as they had no chance for a fire. The young man butterflied out to the cove's edge and dove under the five-foot waves as he hit the open water. I casually gathered the glasses and scanned the scene. The shepherd had found a small bit of wood and was placing it on the beach near the setter, who sat in his customary position. I glanced back and saw the boy in the waves trying to catch some wood collected in a clutter. He grabbed one piece and quickly dropped his head under the waves as the wood bobbed. Scanning back, I looked at the dogs to see the female panting on the shore. The setter came into view as he sprung to his feet, opening his mouth in alarm. Quickly I looked back to the open water and saw a horrifying sight. One oversized piece of wood had separated from the others out near the rocks at the edge of the deep water. The waves were spreading a crimson streak around it, and the color mixed into the turbulent water. The boy was nowhere to be seen.

My reaction was to get help, and I looked for a phone

or staircase. Reality set in as I realized my legs had long been useless and I was a hermit by my own choosing. After several frantic turns, the horror of the situation set in. I was in no position to help, only to observe. There was still no sign of the lad. Then I looked to the beach. The shepherd stood by the shore, spinning nervously and howling out to the lake. In shock I looked for the setter, who had disappeared from the beach. Turning my glasses to the driftwood, I was distracted by something in the water and instantly recognized it as the setter, swimming strongly towards open water, his auburn back cutting a graying wake through the whitecaps. The change of scene startled me for several moments, and I checked the characters again. By the time I came out of the haze of disbelief, the setter had reached open water and slipped under the turbulent seas. For what seemed an eternity the shepherd and I tormented in the situation. She howling and spinning on the beach, and I sitting a continent away watching in horror.

Suddenly the Irish appeared at the entrance of the cove with his mouth wrapped firmly around the boy's wrist. For several minutes he struggled towards shore, constantly resetting his grip on the arm. The German stood onshore barking encouragement in a voice I could hear through the glass. They reached shore and the dog momentarily collapsed in exhaustion. The female hunkered down and squirmed away from her prone master. I fixed my glasses on the young man, and tears began to flow as I saw his fate. Blood flowed from a wound at his right temple, and his color was deathly blue. Nobody could help him now. The setter struggled to his feet and barked a command to the shepherd. The German argued, but only for a second, as the setter bared his teeth and angrily chased her around the south bluff. The setter returned to his master and lay his head gently on his master's neck and began carefully licking his face. He picked his head up once and looked in my direction, then lay his face softly on the cold face of his master. The female returned an eternity later with several people, who gaped at the scene but didn't dare approach due to the warning of the big red dog. They took the body only after the police had joined the friends for eternity with a loud shot.

When you have outlived all your friends and family, death becomes customary and routine. This one was neither of the above, and the pistol shot still rings in my ear. It's said that in every bad situation in life a silver lining can appear. The lining could only be the grays and reds for my paintings. The red was in the setter and in the water that evening. The gray still visits the shore each day in the summer. Each summer night she sits very close to the water, looking west towards Wisconsin. As the sun turns the water and sky red and gray she howls loudly twice and walks slowly around the rocks to the south.

When my agent visited that holiday season he wouldn't buy five large paintings. The first was of the three friends as pups playing, the second of two friends swimming and one watching intensely, the third of a body being brought ashore by a crimson dog. The fourth was of two bodies side by side, with several people, including a pistolled officer, looking on. The fifth depicts the German shepherd sitting close to the shore howling at the water as the sun sets, with two pieces of red driftwood floating and touching the border of the cove and the lake. My agent said I hadn't painted such vivid colors since he'd known me, but the scenes were too macabre for him to sell. I told him the paintings weren't for sale and were to stay in my house over the cove forever. I asked him a question he never has answered: "Bill, what do we really understand of friendship?" He left that day shaking his head in frustration as I returned to mixing reds and grays.

Listening to Ernie

The boarding of the bus was awaited with anticipation of the coming summer adventures as well as relief from oppressive inner-city blacktop heat. With the large military duffel bag stuffed heavy with a summer's worth of clothing and entertainment leaning against my leg I, for the countless time, rummaged through the small carry-on bag for the stack of books and my priceless transistor radio and its earplug. This annual pilgrimage to my grandparents' cabin in northern Michigan had become so ingrained that it would follow me to the end of my own existence. Boarding the bus, I found the most isolated seat available and prepared to bury my nose in one of the many books to be found within my carry-on luggage. During the hustle of the school year, with the restraints of homework and household chores, I always seemed to stockpile several titles for summer reading. As I inhaled the cool, invigorating air conditioning, I waved to Mother and returned to my book and its adventure.

As on most trips north, I tried my best to speak with nobody, choosing instead to isolate myself in the wonderful world of fiction and fantasy. As the bus bumped and lurched over the highways and country roads, my imagination was taken by Twain, Poe, Clarke and Heinlein. The stops came and went, called in a bus driver's monotone, and I slipped comfortably into the places that didn't exist except in another's creation. Shortly after the first extended stop I would gently slip the cherished transistor out of the bag and begin searching.

As the bus rumbled north and the sun moved to my left, I would periodically turn on the radio and sweep the AM band. Searching patiently, I would continue my reading until I found that smooth, lilting voice in the earpiece. For a brief few seconds I would close my eyes and let the words take me away to another place far away. At the first opportunity, with the action stopped, I would quietly replace the books in the bag and gaze out the bus window, reverently listening to Ernie.

The soft southern voice and his vivid descriptions of the action grasped my imagination with the power of creativity. The background noises of the distant stadium only added to his descriptions, like a harmonious accompaniment. The subject was simple; it was always baseball. Never on my trips north had I been disappointed by missing a broadcast; the boys of summer always seemed to be playing on the day of my bus trip. As we crossed the border and proceeded north into Michigan, the game would be painted upon my imagination. As on thousands of other occasions, Ernie would take me to a good place and tell a story that would gradually reach its crescendo in the bottom of the ninth.

"Stanley and McAuliffe on the corners, Kaline awaits the two-two delivery. Line shot headed towards left field— it's long gone, and that's the ballgame," the musical voice was soon calling through the earpiece. Unbeknownst to me, the sun had already started to set and most of the miles were behind us. For several magical hours and two sets of batteries, I felt a friend had talked to me alone, describing more than just baseball.

The bus eased into the country station as I was gathering my things. I placed my transistor and books carefully into the small duffel bag and started to the front of the bus. Looking towards the general store, I could see my grandmother standing on her tiptoes straining to see into the bus. Happiness overcame us as she gathered me close in a hug filled with love. She filled my ears with questions, all the while touching me with a grandmother's affection. Gently, I was guided around the corner of the store to the old red Ford truck idling smoothly with Ernie's and Paul's voices coming from within, a bit too loudly. My grandfather was in his usual place, leaning against the tailgate with his arms and legs crossed. He was already deeply tanned and wore his usual flannel shirt rolled to the elbows with that ancient Tigers cap pushed back on his head. When I was about twenty feet from him he suddenly grinned a greeting and flipped a brand-new hardball at me. To his delight, I caught it deftly and walked to him; he stuck out his hand in a manly greeting and squeezed my hand a bit too tight. As we circled the passenger side of the truck following Grandma, he pulled me to his side and pulled a brand-new Tigers cap over my eyes. He silently released me before she could see us men showing any affection. As he held the door for us, her shy grin and tearful eyes told me of her knowing.

∾

The sun hadn't even awakened when he entered my small room overlooking the lake. His presence was announced more by the odor of his perpetual morning coffee than by any sound. I lay very still as he gently reached under the covers and pulled steadily on my big toe. Grandfather made nearly silent hushing sounds as he handed me my bluejeans and whispered, "I'll meet you at the boat. Bring the tackle boxes."

I dressed on my way to the kitchen, stopping at the refrigerator for a quick slug of milk, straight out of the carton. Tip-toeing down the steps to the basement, I turned the lights out as I left the house, through the sliding glass door. As I reached the door, the image of old Rusty peering in at me caught my eye. Without even looking I reached to the shelf on the left and grabbed a treat for him. He gently took it from me as I gathered the tackle boxes and headed towards the dock, a happy retriever trailing at my feet. Grandfather was in the small fishing boat, holding the dock with one of his powerful hands. He took the tackle boxes from me and held my arm as I gingerly climbed into the boat. When I sat down towards the front, Rusty's padded feet plopped onto the middle wooden seat, pushing the boat away from the dock. In near silence Grandfather rowed the old boat into the pre-dawn darkness.

The silence was not to be broken until after the first fish was landed. This rule was never spoken, but always understood. He rowed with near-effortless strokes around the point and towards the middle of the lake. When we had traveled far enough from shore he pulled at the small Mercury motor twice and it murmured to life, creating a white-on-purple wake in the smooth, black water. When the motor had finally quieted and the boat was coasting, I eased the anchor over and we began to fish. At the moment of dawn I landed a small pan fish, and Grandfather quietly asked, "How do you think them Tig's will do?" As the sun danced over the trees and skimmed away the blackness of the water, we conversed in friendly laughter, both fishing for friendship's solitude.

It was typically mid-morning when we would arrive back at the house. Breakfast would magically be nearing completion by the time we had the gear stowed away and the fish clean. Grandmother would watch for us from the upstairs deck and would begin cooking when she saw us heading for shore. On occasion her morning crossword puzzle would engross her to the point of us seeing her leaning against the cupboard, paper in hand, pencil poised at the ready. Sitting to eat at the old table was as much ritual as could be afforded the three of us. I was too young to realize that every event in their lives was a ritual of schedule.

The three of us pitched in to clean the dishes, with the friendly and casual small talk of the day. Afterwards Grandfather would sit with the morning paper in his favorite old chair on the screened-in porch just off the kitchen. If I was just a bit too slow in escaping to the world of bike riding, baseball playing or friend making, I would hear his deep, loud snore reverberate through the house. Most days I would return for the light lunch and the mandatory half-hour wait with my friends.

We never understood the half-hour rule about eating and swimming, although it was discussed with much seriousness and frustration as we tried to busy ourselves with the preparation of the boat, skis and life-jackets. It seemed like Grandfather would sit at the controls of that old speed boat for hours at a time. Everybody would have his turn and I don't recall anyone ever not succeeding at learning to ski at the beckoning of the master teacher. He never seemed to even have to enter the water, but could teach anyone verbally. His great, deep voice would lose its roughness and turn into a gentle and soothing deepness that conveyed confidence to a tribe of young skiers.

With unknowing willingness, each year I was pulled into my grandfather's world. It was a world of wonder and joy, of happiness and friendship. The routines and constants of his life were few but reverent. Sunday morning church, pre-dawn fishing, mid-morning newspaper napping and listening to Ernie tell of the Tigers' tales. He especially loved the west-coast games that we shared together long after Grandmother had retired for the evening. Together we would listen to the game on the deck while looking through his powerful telescope at the distant constellations. In his quiet tone, the names of the planets and stars were conveyed to me through the years. His voice seemed in harmony with Ernie's and Paul's as they told their stories of what lay before them and what they had seen and learned in their past.

The climax of the summer always came in the last week of July, long after the fireworks of the Fourth had come and gone, before pennant race was to commence. My birthday was a few weeks away, and would be accompanied by the annual summer vacation visit of my parents. It was the only event that the three of us planned together from the start of summer, since planning a daily agenda seemed to go against the beliefs and routines of my grandparents' retirement. The Tigers' schedule was scrutinized and studied with unusual interest. Discussions and disagreements would turn to formulation of ideas and by the first of July we would always be in agreement. Our pilgrimage to the stadium was always two games, either a doubleheader or a night game followed by a matinee. Since my grandfather's retirement from the company, they would only return to the city for this annual occasion. The joy of seeing a ballgame with his only grandson would overwhelm his well-hidden distaste for the congestion, noise and grime we would endure. While we waited for the upcoming games through the Fourth of July, we would celebrate the summer holiday with anticipation of the upcoming pilgrimage.

I now recall the games with great fondness. Although I'm sure it's just in my memory, the Tigers never seemed to lose when we went to the park. Although my recollections are now selective, the weather was always perfect, and although we changed sections each time, our seats were always the best. We arrived early, and stood by the gates at Michigan and Trumbell, just waiting for the ushers to open up for batting practice. Catching a ball was the first priority, and I would tear off for one of the premium corner spots and jostle with the other kids until I had captured one of the stray prizes. My grandparents would already have a mustard-only hot dog and plenty of pop ready for me when I returned to the seats talking of the catch I had made. As I ate, I listened to the two old Tiger fans reminisce about the games they had seen together on this corner all the years past. The names of Gehringer, Colavito, Greenberg, Maxwell and Newhouser were animated with gestures indicating where the ball landed or how a play was made. Many times some of the fans around us joined in and the conversations turned to comparisons of games attended and more plays witnessed.

The first notes of the national anthem always signified the beginning of what most of the fans considered a most solemn event. Silence would sweep over the great old park as the music swelled to its famous crescendo. We always cheered the end of the song, although I could never figure if we cheered the song itself or if we cheered the commencement of the game. The smells and sights of the park are what stuck with me through all the years, but the one sound that could trigger a rush of all the senses was the sound from my small transistor radio that I shared with my grandparents. As we shared the games year after year, they were always accompanied by a chorus of radios, all tuned to Ernie and Paul.

As July fell into August, my birthday would indicate the coming of my parents for their annual two-week vacation to the far north cottage. The times were joyous as we spent the days eating on the lakefront, playing yard games in the evening and boating in the days. For some grandfatherly reason, I was still awakened every morning by a gentle prod, and we made our way to the fishing with the old dog. I thought several times to ask him if we should invite my father for a pre-dawn fishing departure, but these times meant so much to me that I didn't dare jeopardize what I had. Even during the two weeks that my whole family was with us at the cottage, every morning my Grandfather and I would quietly slip the boat out onto the lake, keeping each other company with recognized silence.

As I grew into college age, my time at the lake was cut with my need for good summer jobs. Soon into adulthood, my wife-to-be accompanied me to the lake for the precious holiday weekends, and she soon fell in love with not only me, but with my grandparents and the calm life we led at the lake. With more couples than kids around the cottage, the routines seemed to evolve into different activities with different emphasis. I never understood that the clock of life was speeding along with increasing vigor as the number of times I made it to the lake decreased with each passing year. For some reason, I can recall two daily constants: the Tiger games, and a pre-dawn nudge from Grandfather as the aroma of his coffee announced another early-morning fishing trip.

∽

The whine of the highway was broken only by the seams in the pavement as the big station wagon dipped over them. The call had come during my commute from the city that late July afternoon, and my wife must have shaken silently the way she always does when she cries. My son had been at the cottage for several weeks for his annual visit to his grandparents and great-grandparents. When I came in the side door, spent from the stress of the day and the oppressive summer heat, I knew something terrible had happened. My two daughters and their mother sat silently at the table with identical expressions and reddened eyes. I stood in the door for a moment and nervously twisted my tie loose as I waited for the unusual silence to break. My wife stood and came close to me and whispered through her tears, "It's Grandpa." I sat heavily and hung my head as the tears smeared my glasses. The girls came close and we held each other for several minutes, the tears from all of us falling to the linoleum. Beyond them I could see the suitcases already packed and lined together in the living room. The sameness of all of the suitcases struck me as odd.

The drive seemed eternal, and my mind wandered back to the bus trips of my youth. As the sun began to stretch to the west, the Michigan border appeared before me. The monotony of the drive, lateness of the hour and my un-usual quietness drifted my family into sleep. I savored the sun's last warmth as it set brilliantly to my left. When the car had grown silent except for the heavy breathing, I sud-denly grew restless and reached my left hand back along the door to tap my son awake. He was always good com-pany on long drives, but this time my hand was met by only carpet, and I realized he was already at the cabin. I drove for a few more miles and then reached for the radio dial and started using the seek button. Tuning it softly to my near speaker, I let the instrument land on each station, briefly hoping for some music to soothe my agony. Sud-denly the voice appeared. The pitch and delivery echoed with a vendor's call deep in the background. The radio dial scanned onward, and I pushed frantically at the buttons until the familiar voice came again into the car, filling me with a sense of the goodness of a boy's youth. Although it was my wife sleeping softly on my thigh, I felt for a second as if Grandfather were jabbing me in the leg to make a point about his beloved Tigers.

The west-coast game accompanied me all the way to the driveway, which was crowded with the cars of my sister's family. Once again I listened to Ernie as he pulled me in with his soft accent like an old storyteller sitting on a porch. The names of the players were only familiar in my son's voice, but Ernie took me to a place far away and filled it with goodness and innocence that I had forgotten for so many years. My grief subsided as I remembered the hundreds of games my grandfather and I had listened to together in the perfect coolness of a Michigan summer night. Easing the car into the drive with the lights dimmed, I sat for a moment and listened as Ernie called the ninth for a comeback win.

Although I wore a suit every day at work in the city, it felt especially uncomfortable today. After two long days of entertaining mourners, I had felt confined and had slipped quietly out the door. All that was left was immediate family in Grandmother's old cottage and the new home my father had recently retired to next door. Walking with a pop bottle in my hand, I stopped at the end of the dock, watching the calmness of the lake and listening to the voices of summer vacationers as they echoed to me. I felt his weight on the dock before I heard his approach. He stood close to me from behind and watched the lake with me. "He did good right till the end, son. Nobody recognized anything, and he held his health all the way through. The last night we were listening to the game and he thought those new kids that call the Tigers were Ernie and Paul. And several times he thought your son was you; he kept mixing up your names."

I again felt the tears reach my cheeks as the loss of a lifelong friend stung my heart. He had gone in his sleep, quietly, painlessly and without suffering a sick day in his life. I thought of my son and wondered how he would adjust to his great-grandfather's absence. We stood together as darkness gathered over the cottage and the lake. A queer feeling came over me, and I asked my father, "When did the Tigers get new announcers, Dad?"

"Last year, son. Living out-of-state keeping you way

out of touch, huh," he answered with a chuckle.

I thought hard for several moments about the game I had heard on the drive up several nights before. There was no doubt of who had called the game for me in that car, even though it felt strange Grandfather had heard the same sounds one night before. Twice my mouth opened to share this with my father, and twice it closed before making a sound. I smiled at the special feeling of warmth I felt in the dark coolness of a Michigan night illuminated by scores of constellations.

∽

The coffee aroma stirred me to consciousness in the pre-dawn darkness. I lay quietly and heard the nearly silent shuffling downstairs and a soft murmur of a voice. The lakeside door of my father's house shut quietly, and I could hear him clucking at his old dog as he gathered the fishing poles. Propping myself on an elbow, I strained to hear two floors down. The door again opened, and the youthful strides of my son clumsily tiptoeing across the yard with the tackle boxes brought an excitement to me as I swung a leg onto the cold hardwood floor. The soft arm of my wife embraced my chest and pulled me back as my ears strained for the sounds I had made myself years ago. "Let them be, they need each other now," she whispered kindly to me.

I sat propped for a moment and thought about her statement. Lying back on the bed, I could hear them as they boarded the small boat and loaded their poles and tackle. Father's old dog jumped in, her toenails scraped on the benches and there was a pause. The next sound came as music to my ears as the oars softly cut the still water and splashed gently down, growing softer as the minutes passed.

I lay there sleeplessly until I could hear them no more. The cool dampness of the night still filled the room through the open window, and now I heard new and unfamiliar sounds. From the direction of the kitchen came voices and cupboard doors opening and closing with care. Dressing as silently as possible, I made my way downstairs to the kitchen and kissed my grandmother and mother. They leaned together over the previous day's crossword puzzle and didn't seem surprised to see me. Handing me a cup of coffee as I looked towards the dark lake, my mother said in greeting, "Welcome to the crossword and cooking club, son."

Selling Words

The dawn rituals were paced events that were more invigorating than some people's morning coffee. He would awaken in the back of the van just before dawn, and immediately light a cigarette. The cool rush of tobacco always seemed to clear the cobwebs from his head. Using water and the small tin, he would next brush his teeth, and then eat a quick bit of fruit. The ritual would continue as he opened the van door to the brightness of the day.

Stretching and yawning, he would start the coffee maker and assess the weather for the day. Turning the radio on to the local station, he would uncover the tables with uncommon care and precision. The plastic tarps would be folded and arranged with the practiced movements of thousands of repetitions. Any moisture was diverted to the ground, escaping any hope of contact with the precious books covered by the old tarps. No matter who spoke to him or how many people gathered, he would acknowledge nobody until each and every book was uncovered and all the empty spots were replenished from the van or trailer. Clearing any morning customers, he was soon sitting in the lawn chair, feet propped on the back table, well within reach of the coffee pot. All the chores now accomplished, he would select a book from among the hundreds and turn to a page. He was not the kind of man who ever needed a book mark.

It was the days of the inquiring young minds that gave the only rise to his happily steady life. If the paths of our lives were expressed as line graphs, most would follow a pattern of ups and downs, living for the upward peaks that generally signify moments of happiness or contentment that we search for. Simon lived quite differently along this line graph of life, for it was the straight line he lived for. Any variation in this line was generally met with great apprehension and nervousness. The one variation he gladly tolerated was the occasional appearance of two small children from one of the other traveling flea market booths.

He could recall the first day he saw them, just outside of Copemish. No verbal agreement had ever been reached between him and the brother and sister, but the rules seemed obvious. He was probably the only library they would know until much later in life. There is the memory of the first time they approached his booth with giggles and childish apprehension. With the wariness of their age they looked over the multitude of books, occasionally reaching out to touch one. Holding hands for comfort, they slowly looked over each row of paperbacks, talking very quietly in Spanish. Without knowing the rules or understanding the etiquette, they reverently recognized the international rules of library noise control. After he had spent nearly an hour watching the twins, while seeming to ignore them, they tentatively came towards his seat clutching small children's books in each of their small hands. With a universal gesture of "help yourself" and a small bit a charity in his heart, he waved them away with a small grin. For but a second they paused, and then gleefully returned their change to waiting pockets and skipped away towards their parents' booth across the market.

It wasn't their return a few days, and a few towns, later that surprised Simon. The surprise was that they held the books in their hands. Watching out of the corner of his eye as indiscreetly as possible, he was amazed when the children separated and returned their books to their precise places on the tables. Not many events can cause a lifelong book addict to stop abruptly for such a long period of time. His posture never changed and the paperback didn't move, but his eyes played in each corner as he watched them again go through the lengthy selection process. When the selecting was complete the twins stared at him from across several tables until he acknowledged them with a glance and a grin. They left in a full run, dodging the rows of milling shoppers.

The wind picked up during the day, paralleling the paperback sales. The briskness of the browsing customers kept him busy making change from the sales. Late in the afternoon a lull in the crowd allowed him a few moments to open the small strong box chained to his truck and to organize what he had thrown in during the day into one counted stack of bills. The day's sales were nearly twice that of the average day, and he entertained the thought of checking into a nice motel on his way to Jackson.

"Sir." The intrusion slightly startled him. Recovering, he casually slid the wad of bills into the box and secured it before turning to the voice. A beautiful teenage Hispanic girl stood before him with her parents on either side of her. The father held two paperbacks in his calloused hand. He whispered something into his daughter's ear and waited. In textbook English she spoke, "My father wishes to apologize to you, for he fears that his children have stolen these books from your tables."

Simon waved his hand in the universal denial gesture as he spoke to the pretty black-haired girl while looking at her father, "No, no the twins didn't steal anything. We have an agreement or trade, so to speak. I know the children have the books, and it's okay."

After a pause the girl started speaking to her parents quietly in Spanish. As she conversed with them Simon looked over top of the family's heads in the direction of the twins. They were sitting very close, solemnly looking at the ground in front of a booth that held an abundance of beautiful native Mexican art and crafts. After a few minutes the three-way discussion ended, and the girl turned back to him to translate. "My parents say that if you say it's okay with you, it's fine with them, but they don't understand what type of 'agreement' you could have with my brother and sister."

Simon laughed with his best smile and replied, "I relish the role of librarian to the twins, and in turn I learn much from your children. *Me enseñan español y alegria.*"

They smiled at his attempt at their native tongue, and the mother replied, "*Gracias, señor. Maria y Felix,*" gesturing toward the children.

Simon thought several times during the next day of trying to guide the children's reading patterns, but each time he came upon the same conclusion. For an adult to try to influence the direction in which the young mind wanders is probably meddling and quite possibly more. As the summer's heat intensified and the locations changed every week, Simon saw Maria and Felix read through his children's selection with a growing passion. In an effort to meet the children's parents' supposed obligation, he started making the siblings tell him the titles of their selections in Spanish.

Just before the Fourth of July his young friends came through the dust to his booth set-up in that week's flea market. That very morning Simon had sat with an old and battered atlas. It was indexed with notes written in his cramped handwriting that cross-referenced each town and all the flea markets where he had set up his booth. In less than two months he would have to start heading south to his eventual wintering spot in the Keys. He glanced up from the atlas to refill the coffee cup in time to see the twins. They approached in the early morning dampness, each carrying an end of a large Indian blanket. "Good morning, *niños*," he greeted his visitors.

They giggled and approached, warily holding the beautifully crafted blanket at arm's length. Maria approached, dragging her brother and his end of the blanket with her. "Mama and Papa give to you for fort," she blurted out much too fast as they pressed the blanket to his hands. Simon's mind raced to catch up, but it took them several embarrassing seconds to realize he didn't understand. Felix did not speak, but instead gestured to the American flag atop his van as he smiled shyly and pointed at Simon's neck.

"*Muchas gracias, mis amigos,*" he murmured as they fled. Simon held the blanket as he sat in the chair. Gently he reached into his shirt and rubbed the old dog tags together. They were nearly completely smooth from years of wear.

Southern Michigan summer evenings are a unique experience. The humidity that oppresses in the sunlight gives way to a cool dampness at night. In that flux between day and night called evening, a truly Utopian weather condition exists. This was what called Simon home each summer. This evening he sat in the back of the van above the shores of an inland lake, watching the darkness come over the water. Below him the sound of the lake people drifted up, accompanied by the odors of barbecue and campfires. He had been coming to this spot for most of his life, with the exception of the two years in hell, half a world away. His GI bill had bought the dozen or so acres that nobody else cared about—too far from the water for recreation, too steep for building. He camped occasionally during the early part of the week, and spent the evening of the Fourth here; otherwise it sat desolate the rest of the year.

Darkness had fallen and the parade of boats had begun, the lights and horns of the motor boats piercing the dark quietness of the evening. He smoked quietly until the parade had ended, and snuffed out the smoke when the first fireworks announced the beginning of a traditional event. Simon sat completely motionless as the friendly explosions created a kaleidoscope of colors in the lake and trees. The approving voices of the lake people drifted up to his perch. In the first few years after he came home, the friendly explosions and voices would eventually change into angry explosions and cries of terror; he would find himself back in the hell of the war, fighting a terror called the past. Over the years the terror subsided, but the memories remained. As the grand finale reached a crescendo he again tasted the tears of his memories.

The flea market was at a fever pitch. The holiday weekend and great weather had come together as a record number of sales in all the booths lifted the spirits of the weary merchants. The odd mixture of poor and middleclass people filled the dirt aisles, all dressed in their summer worst. A noxious cloud of dirt, the scent of fair food and human and non-human odors engulfed the grounds, creating a grime probably found in the bazaars of ancient times. Simon manned his booth with resolve, knowing that this weekend could provide his revenue for several months, if not for the year. The tables, which were usually packed, were full of holes from sold paperbacks. He had little time to re-stock and had been reduced to dumping crates of books on the tables by category only. He had refilled his coin changer more times than he could count, and all three strong boxes were stuffed full of wadded bills. The madness had started Friday the fifth and was reaching a crescendo on this Saturday afternoon. Simon counted back change and bagged the books in plain brown bags while pointing out tables and authors and subjects to other customers. Every half hour or so he would see a Native-American article of clothing or household textile in a pair of hands and he found happiness in knowing the weekend's success was finding his friends also.

The day was moving to afternoon, shown by the yellow inferno of sun that was now in his face. Sweat had soaked his bandanna and turned his long hair into thin, slimy strings. It took him more than a few moments to realize something was amiss. The flow of traffic in front of his tables of books had been disturbed. As if a beaver had suddenly built a lodge midstream, the flow was diverted around. Looking up from his books he saw a most revolting sight. Although the features were the same at first, the mirror image he was looking at somehow changed into something very foreign. Standing in front of him was his "identical" cousin. Dressed impeccably in an Italian suit, accessorized right down to the shoes and watch, was Tom. The flea market crowd flowed around his cousin, gawking at him as if a space alien had suddenly landed in broad daylight in rural Michigan.

"What in God's name are you doing here?" he hissed at the image resembling himself but with wealth and status.

"I've brought your shipment of books," his cousin curtly replied.

"No, you pompous fool, you know the contract—the second Tuesday of July at my property," Simon hissed.

"Well, the contract doesn't agree with me. I've brought the driver and van, and my car even has boxes in it, of all things. Now if you don't take the shipment I'll dump it in the parking lot of this god-forsaken pig-slop mud hole," Tom said, calmly wiping the grime away with a white silk handkerchief.

Anger rose in Simon with increasing volume. "So help me, you fool, I'll have you thrown out of here."

Tom moved away from the masses with a look of disgust, "Simon, I'm tired of cow-tailing to this contract of our father's, and by the way, don't threaten to throw me out of a public place, you fool."

Simon grinned widely. Looking over the heads in the crowd he smiled and gestured to the huge face watching the confrontation with great curiosity. A giant of a man wearing torn and worn jeans and a black Harley shirt parted the crowd and looked at Simon from at least two heads above everybody else. His long, graying beard and hair partially covered the tattoos on his arms. "What's up, Si," he growled through his Marlboro.

Simon smiled with irony. "Hey, Pigtail. Need to go to the parking lot for a minute. I don't really trust this guy. Could you keep him here and watch my stuff for a few?"

Pigtail looked Tom completely up and down with a bemused look of disgust. "How 'bout some Cokes?" he said coldly, glaring all the time at Simon's cousin. Tom stood, mouth open in shock at the unfriendly giant standing over him.

Simon cut through the back booths into the parking lot with the effortless, practiced gait of someone familiar with walking through crowds. He spotted the shiny publishing house truck and saw Reggie sitting on the running board, mopping sweat from his forehead. Grinning with increasing width, the overweight driver chuckled at Simon as he neared his resting spot. "Now, the boss boy told you to dump the books, Reg," he teased.

The coal black driver reached into the truck and handed Simon a box of Cuban cigars, still sealed. "Good to see you my friend," he said with just a trace of a Caribbean accent as he patted Simon on the arm.

"What's the scoop, Reggie?" he asked, sitting next to

his father's godson.

Reggie grinned that engaging wide grin. "I got my instructions and even a copy of that contract, and they don't come from that weasel. I'll see you Tuesday, as long as you make breakfast."

Simon rose and presented his hand to the sweating black man. "Love to the family, old friend." Taking the box of cigars, Simon departed, walking by the passenger side of the Mercedes. He dragged the metal corner of the box down the length of the car as Reggie howled with delight.

Simon walked the same direct path to his booth, cutting through the milling crowds and stepping over guy wires that supported the tents and awnings. The purpose and directness of his walking mirrored the intent of his delivery. Cutting through the aisle to his booth he smiled at the twins, who were playing adjacent to their family's display. Simon stepped around his giant, bearded friend and turned to his cousin, who was wearing a look of fear and anger. "You lose, Tom. Now get out of here, and I don't want to see you until Tuesday." His cousin stepped around Simon, completely away from the big biker who stared at him threateningly with his arms crossed over his chest. Simon turned to Pigtail and handed him a six pack of Cokes and opened the box of cigars to his friend. As Pigtail grinned and reached to the box a loud shrill of pain pierced the air. Turning to the sound they saw little Maria in the dirt, holding her petite foot and shrieking in agony. Her twin stood next to her, dumbfoundedly looking between his sister and Tom. Pigtail reached her first, moving with a grace that belied his mammoth proportions. Maria held her arms to him as she recognized the familiar friendly giant she loved to tease in Spanish. Simon caught up to her brother who stood, arm outstretched and pointing at Tom, who stood massaging the ankle he'd obviously turned as he stepped on Maria's fragile toes.

A sudden thunderclap arose from Pigtail's lungs as he turned and bellowed at the one who had inflicted pain on his tiny friend, "Get out of here."

The day dragged to a close, with business suddenly becoming burdensome instead of fulfilling. The Lopezes had taken their daughter to the local emergency room and returned several hours later with a shiny cast on Maria's foot. Pigtail's wife and their elder daughter had taken over their booth, and almost immediately a collection was being passed from vendor to vendor to cover the medical expenses. Simon contributed a crisp hundred dollar bill to the hat and slipped another in his pocket, which he would use to buy her the nicest doll he could find later that evening.

Sunday closed out with a slightly upbeat tempo. Business was good during the day, and Maria paraded through the grounds in a makeshift wheelchair, escorted by her siblings. She carried a pen to each booth and cherished the signatures as much as the attention she received. When they made the circuit later in the afternoon, Simon signed her cast and handed her a brand-new doll, which lit up her face like an angel's. Next they went to Pigtail's booth, were he drew a special caricature of her on the cast. She giggled at him and, of course, talked to him only in Spanish, teasing her friend as she occasionally touched his beard.

Simon closed down his book stands hastily. He had stayed open as long as possible to take advantage of the aisle traffic and upbeat sales. By the time he had folded the awnings and methodically loaded the books into his trailer and van, he had built up a wearisome sweat. Simon made his way around the vendors saying a quicker than usual goodbye, and stopped by the Lopezes' and Pigtail's to compare travel agendas and discuss future flea market rendezvous.

The sun was just moving to his extreme right as he reached the interstate and settled the rig into a steady fifty-two miles per hour. The remembrances of the day left a bitter taste in his mouth that he knew he would have until Wednesday's dawn. The radio was silent and the windows were down, and the drone of the highway cleared his thoughts of all the past events and rolled away the memories. The time schedule he followed so religiously would be kept as Simon saw the sun sink below the western trees in his rearview mirror. Soon he passed through Jackson and exited to the lake.

Simon set up his camp and sat privately under the stars until well past midnight. He reluctantly kicked the fire into submission and retired to his small tent. Sleep, as usual, was preceded by a calming blankness of the mind and spirit. Far off in the twilight of consciousness a dog barked at the stillness of the night.

Well before dawn Simon hit the water down by the public beach. He had bathed and swum for nearly an hour when the beginning of the day was introduced by the first glimmering of light behind the hill on which his property sat. He toweled off and dressed silently, and then retreated to his hill before any eye could be laid upon him. Knowing the day's schedule, he realized that his work would be done well before noon, leaving him plenty of time to go to town for his first good meal in weeks. Within an hour the unloading of the rig had been systematically completed. Simon checked his belongings, starting with a routine inventory of the van and trailer. Everything was unpacked and checked, down to the tape case and maps. He mentally compiled a checklist as he worked his way toward the books and their tarps.

He stopped when he had laid the crates out on the tarps and covered them so very carefully. He took the notebook out of his pocket and made a second list, this one concerning only the books. When he had completed this job his day's work was finished, and he was ready to take the trip to town. The oil change, banking, shopping and nice lunch at his favorite restaurant would consume the rest of the day. Simon returned up the steep trail in the twilight, thankful to be back in his own private environment. Soon after the sun set he retired to the tent and lay in the darkness, listening for sounds he wouldn't hear.

As was his custom, Simon awoke to the stillness of the pre-dawn and lay completely motionless. With his eyes wide open and his ears fully attentive, he waited in this position for the first signs of the day. He thought again of this habit and still couldn't understand whether it was fear or memory that caused it. When the light that preceded the dawn came he deliberately rose and left the tent. He slipped into the ancient Kenny Taylor canvas tennis shoes and skillfully kicked at the cinders in the fire pit. Within a minute the fire was reborn with just kindling, wood and a few practiced breaths. Looking east, Simon saw that the sun was not quite up and he grabbed a towel as he started on a jog toward the lake.

Upon returning from a swim he glanced at the fire, which had grown and now crackled with promise. As he passed by the fire, he set the grate in place and placed a seasoned cast-iron skillet on it. As it heated to fire's temperature, he toweled and changed into fresh shorts and shirt. Pulling supplies from their crates and coolers, he started preparing the breakfast he would share with his friend Reggie and cousin Tom. The coffee was brewed, the pancakes and eggs started, and the bacon near completion when he heard the metal gate creak far down the hill, followed a few moments later by Reggie's truck groaning in protest at the steep incline. Simon smiled with self-pleasure as he realized his breakfast would be completed with uncommon culinary timing.

He had his back purposely turned and his eyes on the food he was dispensing onto plates when they climbed out of their respective vehicles and approached. They stood behind him silently until he stood and handed them each a plate of steaming food. This routine had been played out so many times that words were replaced with expressions and gestures. Reggie's eyes grew wide, and he grinned with the satisfaction of expectations met. He sat quickly in the nearest lawn chair and poked and prodded everything on his massive plate with the intent of finding any missing part of the meal. He was just raising his head in disbelief when Simon placed the coffee mug gently on the ground by his side. Reggie nodded his approval and finally began the slow and tasteful enjoyment of the meal he had waited a year for.

There was no conversation between the three men as they sat in the woods atop the hill overlooking a lake. Simon thought of how funny such a scene might look to an outside observer. The old van and its trailer sat on the edge of the picture with the crates of books, now uncovered, surrounding it. In towards the fire Simon sat facing the other two men. The large black man with the round face held his plate, piled with food, balanced on his legs. His coffee sat perched on the arm of the lawn chair as he ate with deliberate intentions. The other man sat on a napkin covering his chair. He was dressed impeccably in a gray suit and held his food awkwardly, obviously not used to eating without a table. He could not have looked more out of place in the setting if he had tried. In the background were the Mercedes and a large two-axle truck, parked just inside the clearing at the top of the hill. Simon reviewed this image in his mind and drew an accurate picture of it looking from a vantage point behind his van. He grinned at the absurd view he envisioned and thought that no outsider could possibly imagine what was taking place at this breakfast scene.

Simon was still holding his now-cooling tea, his own special blend he bagged every month, watching his cousin intently. Reggie broke the many minutes of silence when he stood and dropped his napkin and paper plate into the fire. This act brought the two relatives to their feet also, and they stared at each other, both trying to win the decades-old argument. "You helping us unload?" Simon asked coldly.

"Not a chance, Si, I have a meeting in Detroit at three. Could you hurry?" His cousin glared at him with cold slate-gray eyes.

"Wouldn't happen to be your wife and kids, would it?'" Simon parried, drawing blood first. At this comment Reggie shook his head sadly, went to the truck, and threw open the cargo door with quick expertise.

"I don't have to take that from you. Leave it to people like you and your ragtag group of friends to throw out an insult instead of complying with a request." Thomas never glanced at him while making this statement; he looked towards the lake through the trees, talking without emotion. "I've grown tired of the games and the charades, Simon. How much do you want for your share of the publishing house?"

The question hung in the air for several moments. All seemed to become still, as even Reggie quieted himself from his unloading chores. Simon stared at the ground for more time than it should have taken, and when he spoke his voice came softly, rising as the words grew, "You'll never understand, will you? To you it's only about possession, power and money, isn't it? If I sold you all of my shares, you think you would be happy, don't you?" By now, unbeknownst to him, Simon was hissing. "So what's the price, cousin? One-hundred grand, quarter of a million, half a million? How high will you go? Come on, let the bidding begin." Fury exploded in his voice and the sound echoed across the lake, breaking the morning stillness. He finished the tirade as his voice returned to him.

Simon spun on his heel and started towards Reggie, only wanting the unloading to end quickly so he could again enjoy his solitude. From behind, a soft hand grabbed him at the elbow and spun him back. "Any of those figures are acceptable, just name your price," Thomas begged with uncharacteristic emotion in his eyes. Simon turned about quickly and faced his only living relation, their noses mere inches away. "How about thirty pieces of silver?"

"What's that supposed to mean?" Thomas screamed, his anger growing by the moment.

Simon suddenly was again silent. Sadness took over his face as he slowly shook his head at his cousin. "How much have you forgotten? What else don't you remember from your past? Sometimes I don't think you're my cousin at all, just somebody who has his body."

"What have I forgotten? What about you? Look at the way you dress, the way you live, your gypsy travels. What have you done with your life, Simon? You had everything, you could have been anything you wanted to be," Thomas screamed again in frustration. "Forget the war, it's been over for nearly twenty years now."

Simon crossed his arms slowly and stared hard into eyes that mirrored his. Instinctively he reached under his shirt and fingered the worn dog tags. He felt the anger and words sucked out of him as flashes of faces went before his mind's eye.

"What would grandfather or our fathers think of you now? They were businessmen who built a company for their families, not for you to turn your back on them and sell books full of meaningless words to the most common of all people from the back of a beat-up Ford van." Thomas' words came more quickly now, as was the family trait. "You disgust me, Simon, almost as much as the vermin you associate with."

The sounds of the boxes sliding down the rollers had increased in speed as the insults hit Reggie and his family. His dislike of one cousin was only paralleled by his respect and love of the other whom he had grown up with and served next to half a world away. His intent now was to finish this job and drive home as quickly as the interstate would take him. This day was uncomfortable every year, but this was the first year it had taken such an ugly turn.

His friend turned slowly towards the lake and said in a barely audible tone, "Well, I guess our disgust is mutual, then." Nothing else was said for a long while as the cousins avoided each other's eyes. Eventually Simon worked his way to the back of the truck and began sorting through the boxes, placing them in location on the tarps for loading into his van and trailer.

The heat and humidity of the summer's day increased as the work progressed towards its conclusion. Near the end of the unloading Simon became distracted again and worked his way over to the bluff, where Thomas stood watching the lake.

He stood there for a long time at his cousin's back looking out over the water and woods. Neither man moved or acknowledged the other's presence, although each was aware of the closeness of the other. The noises of Reggie's labors had ceased before their silence was broken by Simon's voice, which had once again returned to its quiet norm. "I remember a day long ago when we came up here together, the month after you graduated from high school." Thomas never flinched a muscle, not indicating that he had sensed Simon's presence. "We were closer than any friends or brothers then. What I can't figure is if we changed willingly or if life changed us."

He waited a moment for a response but was answered only by silence. "Do you remember that night, Thomas? We came here, just the two of us, and watched the fireworks. We sat and drank the beer we had snitched from Grandpa and talked of the future. You going to college and me and my shaved head going to Asia." For the first time his cousin responded, with a small chuckle, as the vision came to him. "Where did we separate, my friend? Why did we grow so apart and different from those identical cousins?"

Thomas spoke. "We all made choices; me in education, culture and society; you in patriotism, solitude and memories. You remember a single night and point to it as important. Simon, it is not. I choose to grow, live and evolve, and you choose to settle into contentment. Life is about choices and development, Simon. You just never figured it out."

Simon saw the images flashing before him. Years before, on that Fourth of July night, he had stood in this exact spot with his shaved head and proud and regal bearing, Thomas with long blond hair and ragged clothing. Today they stood in the same geographical location, Thomas with the thin, cropped hair and regal bearing, and himself with the long hair and ragged clothing. He looked at his cousin and saw the bitterness and stress that others would surely see as success. His cousin in turn looked at him and shook his head in disgust. The years hadn't bridged the gap, only deepened it with old differences that widened with every spoken word.

Simon stepped quietly around Thomas and stood between the edge of the hill and his cousin.

"What about my offer?" Thomas asked with a sneer.

Simon looked again over the lake and, as he did in uncertain times, reached for the chain around his neck. Suddenly his hand stopped, inches from the dog tags. A grin came to him as he said over his shoulder, "The agreement stands the way it's written." He stroked the blond stubble on his jaw as he waited for the response.

Thomas leaned closer to his back. "You're making a mistake, but that's nothing new."

There was a pause as the gap widened. Thomas turned to leave, but stopped and parried one last time. "By the way, I was thinking that your bit of land here would make a great condo development."

Simon raised his voice to the lake for all to hear. "Not even for your thirty pieces of silver, cousin!"

A Glimmer in the Storm

"A hundred and twenty-four years, I figure, Jas." The heat off the barrel-wood stove felt like the breath of Hades compared to the sub-zero temperatures outside of the badly dilapidated old warehouse.

"I'm afraid to ask, Cons," I stammered through lips cracked and dry from the wind and the cold.

"Ah, young friend," he offered, guiding me by the elbow to the frosted window overlooking the eastern straits. He sipped the liquid from his dented and aged silver flask and pulled off a tattered glove with his remaining teeth. Rubbing at the easternmost window with the now-bare hand, he motioned through the hole in the frost at the distant islands.

"A mere century and a quarter before they choke thes' her' strait with those Christmas trees," he mused, peering through the ever-shrinking hole in the frost.

Suppressing a grin, I answered, "Cons, that's just a bit beyond our time, eh?"

Constantine spun to his aged stove, opened the door, and stirred at the fire. "Just last year the big ferry tangled one of the trees in her port prop. A bloody expensive mess it was, laddy."

Looking about the old warehouse I tried to count the pints and quarts that hadn't been there my last visit.

Among the grain, crates, general merchandise, equestrian supplies, wood and stoves I could find three quarts and five pints I didn't recognize. They all had the customary swallow left at the bottom of the bottle. Pulling one of the fascinating yellowed nautical charts from the floor, I bit, "How did ya come up with one hundred and twenty-four years?"

He began explaining his computation, jabbing his finger in the air. "Son, understand I's been watching them standing those trees in the ice since your daddy was haulin' da bales across. Figure the trees are 'bout four feet high and seven feet round reducing a bit for water rot. Figure in the fathoms and calculate the years past and the rest comes easy. Son, in a hundred and twenty years you'll be walking the bales to the four-leggers over there on fudgie heaven." He smiled a schnapps-induced grin through jagged and neglected teeth.

"Ah, Cons," I ribbed, "at least they mark the trail and accomplish something."

He spat on the stove, setting it to sizzling. "Boy, there bein' no use except to hazard the boats. If'n you can't find your way in these straits, you don't belong here. If you need directions out there, you better be hoping for a miracle."

"Cons, it's turning nasty. Let's get her loaded," I urged. He only muttered to himself as he stoked and shoved wood into the aged stove. I slipped out the small side door and walked through the drifting snow to the pick-up. As I pulled up to the south door with RECEIVING painted onto the weathered trim, I could only snicker at my father's observation about Cons. "Too many years on those ore freighters will do a man's mind a strange turn. You're lucky he doesn't talk to the bales."

The big Arctic Cat, with the flat sled on two tapered runners, sat in its accustomed spot about two feet from where I'd have to pull the hay wagon. Putting the Ford into first gear, I slowly pulled the wagon parallel to the sled on the first try, about three attempts fewer than my average.

Cons came through the side door and leaned into the building, breaking the wind to light his pipe. I began the systematic process of loading the hay and straw from the truck's wagon onto the sled. The awkwardness of the doubled wool gloves, layers of thermals and snow suit only accented the stiffness from last night's game. I worked quickly, trying to stretch out by breaking a quick sweat. In the rhythm of throwing the bales, I glanced at Cons with amazement. I was not looking for help because handling the bales with seven fingers and only one thumb made the work far too clumsy. It was nearly fifteen below zero, and I was bundled in about every piece of apparel available in a dry-goods store. My elderly friend had on only a threadbare sweater, open Mackinaw coat, worn mitts, and no hat. He seemed impervious to the cold with that skin, weathered enough to make the Ancient Mariner blush the shade of a sixteen-year-old Ice and Snow Festival Queen's frosted cheeks. The crooked nose, thick wavy hair and mysterious, distinguishable ear-to-chest scar only added to his appearance.

"Heard you played a decent game las' night," he murmured, his voice cutting the wind with a shrill pitch.

"Rough and tumble without no breaks from those hometown refs," I replied.

"Don't expect any less from them, either. How did ya do?" he asked, searching for a conversation to which he already knew the answers.

"We won by a dozen, and I got twenty-seven and twelve boards. Thought we'd have to stay down below. The bridge patrol escorted us across before they closed the Mac down."

"Ah, just a nice January night lad; was nothing more than a breeze."

"Coming to see us play the Saints next Friday?" I asked him, already knowing he wouldn't stray from his familiar spot in the near corner of the gymnasium. He didn't drive, so he cherished the handful of times a year he could see me play. The old-timer had known my family for three generations, and me since I was old enough to explore the old docks and warehouse on my toddler's legs.

"Ah, to tell, laddy. Talk about town is that they're going to kick your pretty hayshaker arse back up the lake," he grinned.

I couldn't let it pass for both our sakes. He had never let me forget how much money he had collected on the previous home game in December. "Yeah, old sailor, about like the last time. If I remember, they tore me up to the tune of a twenty-point thumping and held me to thirty-two points."

He outright cackled while teasingly rubbing ice from an eye to indicate the scar I had received from an intentional elbow during that game. "At a price, my pretty friend. Maybe you'll pay more this time, eh? At least that's what the Stepenski cousins have been boastin' all over town."

The bales were dropped onto the sled with Constantine prodding them into place as best he could with his feet. The fifty-eight-pound bales began to lighten under my shoulders as the stiffness finally left my body. With practiced expertise we stacked the bales into a level and sturdy load pattern.

Cons limped around to the front of the sled and fired up the big Arctic Cat with a few brisk tugs. She sputtered, roared and kicked out pre-mix gas as he played the idle. I jumped gingerly down from the top of the completed load and slipped in the side door, prancing to the old stove for the last bit of heat I would soak up for some time. Cons followed me in shortly, without even bothering to brush the snow from his face and neck.

Cons passed by me at the stove and opened a very old sideboard. From the sideboards' cluttered inside he carefully chose a bottle of schnapps and poured a little into the flask. He swirled the liquid about before casually dumping it out; he then filled the flask and sealed the top. He came back to the old stove and spit a stream of liquor onto it, setting it to sizzle with protesting violence. He handed me the bottle while slipping the small metal flask into the pocket of my parka. I took a short drink of the schnapps while he grinned and muttered something about "antifreeze." The old-timer looked me directly in the eyes and said with a bit of seriousness, "Be careful out there laddy. I'll see you off."

I mounted the big sled and turned to my friend, saying goodbye with a quick left-handed salute. The big black Cat barked and roared in protest, belching black smoke from its short pipe. With strained effort she crept down the ramp toward the lake. I stood straddling the seat, pushing my weight to the back of the track, aiding the snowmobile's labored efforts. I steadily increased the pressure on the accelerator, and the machine and sled dipped off the ramp onto the ice. I cautiously scanned the load of bales, watching the key points on the corners for the telltale signs of dumping the load. The load rocked but stayed stable as the sled came onto the ice, settling nicely when I hit the path on the lake, worn smooth from the variety of vehicles and humans traveling to fish or visit the islands. Glancing back beyond the fumes and load of hay, I could see Constantine standing near the shore. Blowing snow was whipping around him, obscuring his legs as he waved me off. The chiseled face, battered, windblown clothes and legs obscured by snow gave him a strange, ghostly appearance. A chill ran up my spine, caused by more than the brisk northwesterly breeze. I moved forward in the seat, settling in before the blast of ice-cold wind hit me in the back, as it came unimpeded across the flat ice.

Each year the locals from the north side of the straits would take their Christmas trees and line a trail over to the island. The trees are generally placed about thirty feet apart and spaced diagonally about every forty paces or so. The uniquely marked trail became the main "road" until the late thaws that broke the ice. In order to enter the "road" it was important to position the sled long before I reached the trees. Due mainly to my rig's lack of maneuverability, I made the necessary adjustments and kept slowly increasing the throttle until I passed the first marker, running a course dead-center between the trees.

Turning to check on the stability of the sled, I was careful to fill my built-in systems with information. Often on this solitary journey I would imagine myself a pilot on an important flight. The rituals of these trips were down to nearly perfected checklists and routine duties. When I turned for my usual load check, something other than the load caught my attention. The sky back toward the mainland had turned a surreal purple and gray. Being somewhat protected by the stacked hay, I wasn't completely aware of the wind as it gathered snow and swept it across the lakes.

As I looped around the first tree and headed down the road toward the island, I stood tentatively on the sideboards of the snowmobile and looked closely at the surface of the ice. The January thaws hadn't left any major cracks in it. The route ahead gave me the impression of a vast desert lying before me, the three islands shimmering oases in the distance. Glancing behind, I again looked at the westerly sky with puzzlement. Every soul who lives around the northern lakes soon inherits the ingrained habit of monitoring the weather. Never in my life had the horizon turned such an ominous purple-gray. The westerly sky had suddenly taken life and seemed to metamorphose every single second, but into what, I didn't know.

Trying to put my concerns about the rapidly changing weather into the back of my mind, I turned back to the tree-lined trail. Scanning the few gauges on the Cat I saw that the fuel indicator was moving at its usual quick downward pace. The other gauges reached to their maximum points, showing the unusual and heavy strain the weight of the hay put on the old snowmobile. I slowly settled into the steering column of the Cat; huddling close to the windscreen gave the impression of warmth. As I reached the halfway mark, keeping as warm as possible became my first priority.

Settling into a cocoon-like stillness, I waited until the break in the pattern approached. On each side of the road were groupings of three trees placed directly across from each other. This point, about one mile from the island, annually marked the visual triangle between the two smaller islands and mainland. Reaching out, I found the headlight switch from memory and began turning it on and off repeatedly for about ten seconds. The blowing snow was covering the shoreline and I didn't bother to look for a reply. Aunt Lydia had been rung and was patiently watching the one-mile point to get everything ready, just as she always has. Coming closer to the island brought only a thought that no matter how commercial and populated this island was in season, the winter still belonged to the elements. The dozens of houses and businesses lining the docks and western shores were not even visible until a scant half-mile from shore. They were completely owned by the snow and ice and seemed to lie in a living, changing state. I hadn't visited the island in-season much recently, although I had been across at least two dozen times in the last few years. The sights, sounds and feelings of the quiet off-season just could never be matched by anything man could achieve.

Coming into the shoreline I throttled the big Cat back and tweaked the choke to increase its richness. Experience had taught me that momentum and angle, not speed, were the keys to getting across the ice bridge and onto the island. With the impending weather and soreness from last night's game, I had no desire to handle the bales another time.

With my head cocked to look both forward and aft, I rocked across the ice bridge and watched as the hay careened first right and then left, pausing precariously at a critical angle before settling back into position. Moving a block off the shore, I slowly exhaled with relief. I followed the worn trail through the ghost town and swung wide in front of Uncle Lynn's stable just as he opened the second large door with his usual crooked grin.

The Cat coughed and sputtered in protest as I shut her down and stiffly crawled off the machine. Lynn tossed a look at me, calling, "You'n look pretanear froze to the bone, hayseed."

I laughed at the old and worn line as I drew the thick liquid out of Cons' flask. Lynn secured the huge rolling doors and met me at the wood stove. Taking the flask he made his usual remark about my age and mother, as a stirring from the back of the stables increased in intensity and volume. I squinted into the dim depths of the stables, whistling in a soft monotone. Lynn laughed. "Go ahead nephew, your girlfriends await. I'll unload."

Thanking him, I strolled slowly toward the sounds as a dozen eyes shone back in anticipation. Cutting right, I approached the stanchions as two huge heads descended upon me. From above my six-foot four-inch height two lively females buried me in love. With remarkable gentleness for beasts of nearly a ton, they licked, nibbled and nuzzled my face and neck for a glowingly warm eternity. Reaching around each of the Clydesdales' heads I slowly started scratching behind their ears. "And how are Lady and Lovey today?" They responded with soft whinnies and cooing.

With distinct personalities, more so than many humans, they fell into their parts quickly. As I moved into the stall Lady gently moved me against the stanchion and leaned her massive shoulder onto my chest and pinned me. I held very still as she looked passively around and winked at me with her eyelashes fluttering across my cheek. Meanwhile Lovey was shaking me down with the dexterity of a New York mugger. Her nose rummaged through my pockets looking for what she knew was there. With one hand I held up a piece of rock candy in front of Lady and she eased the pressure with a wink of gratitude.

Meanwhile the shakedown from Lovey was reaching a frantic pace. I moved closer to her while scratching her ears and made another piece of hard candy appear next to her nose. With both of the Clydesdales content, my routine continued as I greeted the other four horses. Moving to the wood stove, I warmed myself as Uncle Lynn finished throwing off the bales.

My mind wandered as I looked at the rows of empty stalls. On the few summer visits I had made to the stables, every stall was packed with horses either coming in or going out to drag the tourists around the island, either in carriage or on their backs. The Fudgies invariably returned home telling of majestic rides and their expert handling of the mounts. Most never realized that the horses knew every inch of the island; you could literally drop the reigns and they would tramp around the memorized path, pausing for a moment at each scenic spot.

I again thought of the day I accompanied a friend with a youth group from down-state. Being the person who handles all of Uncle Lynn's mounts at their regular weigh-ins, I had become a familiar friend to the horses. Rest assured one they loved, due to the sweet bribes I used to help move their considerable weight. On this particular day I was enamored with a young filly from the youth group and was not aware of my surroundings. As we walked up the hills toward the hotel I became aware of all the Fudgies pointing down the hill behind me. Turning on my heel, I smiled at the sight of at least fifteen of my uncle's horses following me in a pack. No matter what commands or pleas the riders gave, the horses just crowded closer to me, the nearest one being within a few feet.

As often is the case, the tranquillity of such a scene was broken in an instant. Around the front porch of the hotel and down the hill came Baby in a defiant strut. Baby, sleek black and a full sixteen hands, was her own horse. Lynn kept her as the last horse in the stable, generally only for use by the two of us and a few experienced stable hands. This day a rich, spoiled seventeen-year-old and her harping mother had badgered my exhausted uncle into letting the "experienced" equestrian beauty take the last available horse on the island.

When Baby spotted me and her stablemates she was a full hundred yards up the hill. Already she was twitching her head in anger and her nostrils were flaring incessantly. A whining teenage voice nagged at Baby as the rich girl spurred her again, against ribs probably already bruised. For the first time Baby responded to this rider. With a snort of recognition to me she leaped to her hind legs, paused there and then bounded several yards down the cobble hill in my direction. A fully sprinting horse can cover that short distance in a matter of seconds, even while spinning, kicking, jumping and biting at the obstruction on her back. Chaos reigned in the next few seconds, making them seem like days. Down the steep hill she bounded, while Ms. Rich Equestrian pulled her ears, yanked her mane, slugged her neck, cursed at her and raked the beautiful horse with her riding boots. As the priss held on at precarious angles, Baby cleared the narrow road and sidewalks with wide-sweeping legs and reckless spinning abandon. Tourists and workers alike dove into shrubbery and flower gardens, causing hundreds of dollars of damage. After a pause I instinctively raced up the hill toward the chaotic scene, calling to the excited horse. As the gap narrowed, Baby's back foot caught the curb's edge and she stumbled head down onto me as I held tight and forced her head to my stomach, shielding her eyes. For a brief moment the huge animal went completely still as I whistled to her softly. My actions forced Ms. Priss to finally lose her balance and tumble from the calmed horse, scraping and tearing her way down the hill sans mount.

The calm I forced upon myself was flowing to my huge friend, and she seemed to accept it momentarily. Suddenly the bloodied girl flew at the horse with an unequaled rage, kicking her back legs repeatedly. Baby reacted with purpose this time. Each time the toe of that riding boot struck her leg, she kicked and lunged at her assailant. Being attached to her neck, I went for a ride no thrill-seeker would ever appreciate. Spinning wildly, my feet completely elevated, I searched for my elusive equilibrium. Suddenly Baby backed away and hunkered down; using this to my advantage, I twisted her head and laid her down very gently. She didn't move as my friend came over and lay across her neck. Then I saw the blood streaming from the horse's back legs. Her rage jumped to me and I spun around in time to see those boots raised again to strike the downed horse; it never happened as my foot struck first. Over and over I kicked her back up the hill toward the exclusive hotel. I kicked the girl first in the legs and then in the butt as I screamed obscenities over and over. My rage turned to tears as I finally returned to Baby. Tearing my shirt in two

I wrapped her back legs carefully. My friend told me later that the dozens of witnesses had applauded wildly, but I never heard a sound. I was told I just hissed, "Get away" to anyone who came near. Trailing blood, with Baby's head buried in my side, we limped back to Uncle Lynn's stable.

My daydream jolted. "If you are gonna grin all day, I'll hafta ask if she's pretty."

"Oh, a true beauty," I responded. We paused to look at the bulletin board near the customer desk. With a cut credit card, thousands of dollars in vet receipts, pictures, a vet's description of Baby's lameness and the island paper's article on the incident, the value of the horses was clearly spelled out. Lynn laughed and tapped the end of the article, which read, "The young lady's attorney will surely be puzzled by a wide variety of witness descriptions of her assailant, which include a midget, a blind man, a knight in shining armor and yes, a jolly green giant." Nick, the local constable, had recorded every witness's account in detail, but strangely none seemed quite accurate.

Uncle Lynn murmured, "I still say the jolly green giant one is perfectly accurate. How about up to the bar for some of your Aunt Lydia's fried goat eyeballs?"

I laughed and commented, "They seem to suit you," as I tapped his expanded belly. One of the joyful bonuses of coming across the lake was experiencing the nurturing of Aunt Lydia. Being childless herself, she took great pride in spoiling me with food and attention. By far the greatest secret of the island was Lydia's Grill, the bar and grill housed on the lake side of the upstairs of the stables. Although no place was completely tourist-proof, Lydia's was close. With no advertising and only a small alley entrance, the quaint place was a refuge of sorts for the natives of the island. In the winter the spectacular seasonal view was an added bonus to the simple menu and good company offered at my aunt's grill.

As it was closing in on supper time, about half of the island regulars were already in the bar, playing pool and telling stories. As Lynn and I entered, greetings from one and all abounded and Nick cleared my customary place at the end of the bar next to Lydia's work station. I was greeted heartily by Lydia with a kiss and an overly generous helping of baked chicken and dumplings. Within minutes the small talk was over and the conversation turned to the relevant topic. Basketball dominated the winter months, followed by ice fishing a distant second. The men grilled me on our schedule, made predictions and teased me about my slender build. Alliances ran deep to certain teams, but the whole group accepted me as family and was more than willing for any tidbits from "our star."

As the gay atmosphere bounced around me and I started on the apple pie, my gaze turned more and more often to the straits. Once again visibility had obscured most of the landmarks, but I was troubled by the strange purple-gray glow in the sky. After a few minutes my Uncle Lynn commented on how strange the weather seemed. The murmurs from the group all seemed to agree with that statement, and I fidgeted slightly. Lydia came close and smiled while offering steaming hot chocolate and seconds on the pie. I hesitated, but she raised an eyebrow, and I smiled and dug in so as not to offend her.

My aunt hovered over me watching me devour the food. Below my feet, which were propped on the bar's foot-rail, a small puddle was forming from the snow melting off my boots and snowsuit. I finished the pie, to my aunt's delight, and peeled away the top of the snowsuit, letting it hang at my waist. The pool playing stopped as I approached the table and the big, red-headed man shouted in the general direction of the bar, "Lynn, were you ever as skinny as your nephew here, or was you always fat as a toad?" Laughter sprinkled around to everybody as Lynn squeezed my shoulders with his strong hands.

"Jas, we're hoping the ice will hold so we can make it
to the mainland for the tourney in March," another pool
player stated. "If not, we may have to shut this Fudgie trap
up and head inland beforehand."

Their talk continued about the local high school basketball that so engulfed all of our lives. While the quarreling
and wagering proceeded I slipped over to the big picture
windows and gazed at the straits. The bridge and connect-
ing towns had all but disappeared from sight in the waning
afternoon. An occasional light poked through the sky,
which was growing increasingly murky and strangely blu-
ish-purple. I looked over to Lydia, who was cleaning the al-
ready-immaculate bar. Talking in a hushed tone that only
she and I could hear, I asked, "Aunt Lydia, would you turn
on the weather report from your marine?" She glanced up
and looked past me at the snow-covered ice. With a very
slight furrow of her deep eyebrows she reached under the
bar, flicked on the weather radio and turned its volume to a
low level so as not to disturb the growing crowd around the
pool table. The two of us listened intently as we watched
the wind whip snow toward the island. As the announcer's
recording started over for the third time, I felt my Uncle
Lynn's presence very close behind me. He listened with us as
he watched out the window, reading the weather with a
practiced intent. Touching me very gently on the inside of
my elbow, he led me away from the corner of the bar and
toward the windows. "Maybe you should stay here to-
night," he said with a seriousness that was strange to me.

I looked out at the ice for an extended moment and
shook my head slowly. "Dad's down in Saginaw with the
truck. I'd better go close up and make sure everybody is
okay at home."

My uncle looked hard at me, judging my decision by
watching me.

He nodded with that uncharacteristic seriousness. "Let's get you going then. Kiss your aunt and say your goodbyes. I'll be in the stable." I kissed my aunt and thanked her for the food. She hugged me a bit longer than usual. I walked through the room and paused at the pool table to say farewell. Looking back to the bar I saw that Lydia had her back turned to me and had turned off the radio. I smiled at the ribbing I took from the island people and ribbed them back when they good-naturedly called me hayseed and flatlander. Making my way to the stable exit, I picked up the bag of molasses cookies on the banister and took one look back out the windows. An ominous bank of purple clouds choked the straits and seemed to be rolling from the top down to the lake. I jogged down the steps toward the stable with many thoughts on my mind.

Entering the stable I saw Lynn had pulled the hood and seat off the sled and was rummaging in all the compartments. A blue smoke hung in the stable from exhaust, telling me he had already checked the sled over mechanically. All the emergency provisions were out, and he had checked each one over in the beam of the flashlight he held as he saw me approach. "You had better see your girlfriends. I want you to leave soon." I walked over to the stable, and the stillness was broken by the rustling of large horses. I fed each horse a bit of cookie, saving the biggest pieces for Lovely and Lady. They nuzzled my neck with tenderness and accepted the cookies with gratitude. I kissed them and stroked their long chins for a moment before I turned to leave. As I stepped away a jolt stopped me, and I realized that Lady was holding my hood firmly in her mouth. Smiling, I convinced her to release it and kissed her nose once more before returning to the sled.

I arrived to the sound of the snowmobile firing as Lynn again pulled the starter and played with the throttle as blue smoke belched and clouded my way toward the doors. All the gear was stashed away and oil and gas cans sat nearby, indicating that the tank had been topped off. He had adjusted the idle and stepped towards me as I approached the sled. Uncle Lynn looked deep into my eyes and handed me the old helmet as I finished pulling on my face mask. He grabbed me around my ribs in a near hug of affection. "You be careful out there, skinny."

I looked over the sled to the trailer pushed into the corner. Shaking my head, I leaned close and raised my voice above the rumbling Cat. "He ain't gonna like me coming back without it."

"Tell ol' Constantine he'll get it back as soon as the weather clears. Now get out of here. Stay within the Christmas trees, and call your aunt as soon as you hit shore, skinny," he said pushing me to the sled. Lynn walked to the doors and waited as I adjusted my helmet, visor, gloves and mittens. I revved the engine and turned on the lights, waiting to hear the idle before nodding to him to open the doors. He pulled back the doors and the wind and cold rushed at me as I eased the powerful snow machine out of the stables. The storm engulfed me immediately, and I gunned the throttle as I ducked behind the windshield and started down the street. I looked back before turning the corner and saw Uncle Lynn outside the doors, framed by the lights of the stable. He raised his hand slightly in my direction just before a flurry whited out his image in my faceshield.

The sled moved freely without the cumbersome bulk of the trailer, and I stood on the rails as it bounced powerfully through the small drifts that completely obliterated my tracks made just over an hour ago. I hit the shoreline and crossed the ice bridge in the air, unleashing the engine's power as I molded into her steering column. The storm had increased greatly in intensity in just the past few minutes, squeezing the visibility to maybe fifty feet. I looked for the first trees with confidence as they broke through the whiteness, looking like lonely green sentries. Wrapping the sled around the first trees, I quickly passed a few others and slowly altered my course to the northwest and settled into the seat, steadying the accelerator. I checked my gauges with satisfaction and looked up to the sky to see only snow and the growing darkness of the storm and evening.

I pulled on the right side of the steering column very slightly as the trees took a northly curve toward shore. The wind was pushing hard against the snowmobile, rocking it with irregular jolts of violent energy. Turning my knees inward and standing slightly, I strained to see the approaching trees through the growing whiteness that engulfed me in its folds. This whiteness was framed by black as the storm unleashed its violent intentions on the straits with all the fury it had gathered as it barreled across the big lakes. Storms were commonplace in my young life, but never had I felt as exposed and threatened as I did now. Leaning over the windshield, I looked forward with the ray of the headlight and saw only whiteness and snowflakes packed so close together that they reflected the light back toward me. My line of sight ahead was completely obstructed, and I quickly checked my peripheral vision for the trees that had been streaming by. My subconscious had been noting the trees as they passed, but to my horror I could no longer see the dark objects on either side as I powered onward. Turning my head quickly to the right, I stared hard into the contrasting white and black and saw nothing past the end of my arm's length. I wrenched my head the other way and saw the same white darkness that now seemed to surround my whole world. My mind raced with the possible consequences of any action I might try. The speed of the visions was quickly paralleled by the thought of how any mistake would be magnified so many times over.

How long? The question hit me suddenly. The trip was just over five miles and usually took about twenty minutes in fair weather. Without the trailer I was cruising at a good clip, and I figured I was more than five minutes out, which should put me just under halfway to the mainland. Instinctively I released the throttle when a mental map of the straits popped before my mind. Another fear gripped me as the thought of burying the snowmobile in the terrible conditions caught me, and I thumbed the throttle forward far enough to sustain some momentum. The map on Con's table appeared again, and I mentally swung a compass needle out from the island two miles and realized my fears. If I had veered too far south or north by just fifteen degrees or so I would hit the shipping lanes to my left or the open water to my right in a few short minutes. Straddling the seat with my leg, I dragged the other foot in the snow, gently easing it down. I could feel the fresh snow kicking over my boot for several inches until my foot hit a solid plane and jumped several times across the surface. Deducing that the January thaw had left the snow hardened, I pulled my hand off the throttle and let the Cat coast to a stop. She settled about a half a foot downward at the end and finally came to a rest, her quiet rumble being my only companion on the darkened ice.

I carefully looked about and realized the visibility was indeed just a few feet. Turning myself around backward on the machine, I looked back in the direction I had come and saw the last traces of my path as a gust a snow covered it before my eyes. I sat still for a moment, listening and looking in the direction I thought the island was, hoping to see some lights. Nothing. Keeping my hands secured to the seat for fear of becoming detached, I turned slowly to my left and strained my ears and eyes into the distance. When I had rotated to the front of the machine, my heart stopped completely. The only sense alerted was my hearing, which was filled with the sound of the howling wind. Reaching down, I killed the lights on the sled, removed my helmet, and waited for my eyes to adjust. I sat for what seemed like a long time, scanning the quadrant in front of the sled, looking in vain for the bridge lights. Again nothing. I killed the snowmobile, hoping for help in the silence.

Fear crept into my body, joined by the unexpected rush of an emotion that accompanies strangers to our presence. The scenarios played through my mind quickly as I tried to push logic to the forefront of my thought processes. To venture any farther would take me into an unknown direction with a good chance of finding open water. If I went into the water I would perish within minutes, even if by rare chance I could struggle back onto the ice. If I sat there and waited out the storm, I would gamble on the fact that it would blow itself out. I estimated the temperature to be just below zero, and with no shelter from the gale-force winds, the wind chill must have been at least fifty below. For the first time since I had been loading the hay and straw on the sled, I ignored the equipment and did a quick system check on my own body. Even with the layers of clothing, the cold had started to penetrate, and I could feel its icy grip in my extremities. Deep inside of me I could feel the fear slowly die. My stillness on the seat was a mirror opposite of the wild wind and snow that was giving strong signs of the breath of life to the storm.

The disappearance of my gloves beneath the white accumulation snapped my attention back. I had seemed to drift to a place of quiet and warm content for what must have been several minutes. Through the deep contrast of darkness and the storm's whiteness I saw only the evergreen of the Christmas trees in my mind. Looking over my shoulder in the opposite direction of the nose of the big Cat, I tried to calculate the minutes and seconds that had passed since I had passed the last tree. Less than a minute had passed as I had sped on, reading gauges and squinting into the storm. Thirty miles an hour, fifteen miles in a half an hour, about a half-mile in a minute. Again I tried to fix my position on the map burned into my mind. Any direction I motored in could lead into open ice and water as well as landfall. To sit there waiting out the storm could be fatal, because the storm might last all night, leaving me to freeze on the ice.

My heart suddenly stopped. The sound reverberation reached me about the same time as the ice popper exploded around me. Instinctively I grabbed the handlebars of the machine as the phenomenon subsided into the storm. Nearly every trip I heard these loud sounds, caused by the ice moving under its own pressure, but it hadn't scared me since the first time I had heard it. With a glaze of fear-induced sweat, I twirled on the machine and popped open the seat, groping through the emergency supplies that Uncle Lynn had checked over. Fumbling over the equipment, I removed my gloves, placed them carefully under my legs and plunged my hands back into the hidden compartment. The cold cylinder of the flashlight and stiff coil of rope were easily identified in the midst of the other tools and supplies.

I paused for a second to plot out my direction. Stowing the rope over my shoulder and placing the flashlight in my pocket, I closed the seat on the old Cat and pulled her starter twice before she sputtered to life. For once I was grateful for the faulty exhaust and loud characteristic roar as she settled into a rough idle. Quickly I moved to her rear tow bar and tied a quick loop knot over the bar, pulling on it twice to test its strength. Uncoiling the rope into the snow, I felt for the opposite end in the darkness. The nylon zipped through my raw, callused hands as I counted arm lengths and guessed the end to come at around one hundred feet. Pulling the last two feet, I started to force the stiff rope into a hand loop when a fearful thought creept into my mind. In a flash my imagination created a scene of the sled crashing through the ice and the loop tightening on my wrist and pulling me to the bottom of the frozen lake. The imagined sight of this possible fate stunned me briefly. Recovering, I instead tied the end into a large clumsy knot several times over itself until it was the size of my fist. Holding my finished creation between my knees I replaced my gloves and mitts, pulled the large flashlight out, and placed the knot end of the rope in my hand.

With effort I flipped on the light and felt a brightening as a beam hopefully jutted into the void. I backed away from the sled and guessed the flashlight's effectiveness at about six feet, but diminishing in the frequent gusts. Without a conscious decision I lurched to the right smiling at what my coach would call a bad basketball habit of going to your strength. Stumbling through the snow I sensed the rope uncoiling as I fanned the light back and forth, aiming toward what I wildly guessed to be south. Probing further, I counted twenty small steps and felt a slight give as the ice accepted my weight. Standing motionless, I peered hard to my right, straining to see any color of light that would indicate the bridge. Nothing. Bad habits, bad instincts. The Bible story came quickly to me, cast your net on the other side. *Go to your left,* my coach seemed to plead.

I started to follow the rope carefully, but as the texture of the ice and snow turned again more solid, I felt my hands groping in a hasty fear. Turning my head slightly, I heard the rumble of the sled and staggered the last few feet to it holding a limp rope. Without pause, I touched the seat and started to the other side, holding the flashlight at arm's length. I set each foot down carefully, judging the texture of the frozen matter underneath. After less than twenty small steps, the energy of the storm drowned out the idle of the sled, and the wisdom of my idea dimmed.

As I passed the fortieth step I realize the rope was shortening to its end, and I stopped counting steps. Moving more slowly, I increased the arc of my flashlight sweeps until they spanned nearly one hundred and eighty degrees. Nothing but the snow's whiteness surrounded by the eternal darkness. My left arm pulled backwards and I stopped with the awareness of being at the end of the rope. Turning I pulled hard and felt the rope give a few more feet as I mentally pictured it jumping out of the snow and pulling tight a few feet in the air. Turning back to the darkness, I stretched my left arm against the rope and held the light outstretched in my right hand, leaning against the weight of the sled and turning slowly in a semi-circle. On the first pass I saw nothing, and I swung back, raising the light up just a bit more until it was even with my chest. There! In the far reaches of the light something twinkled. Holding on to my precarious posture I moved the light ever so slightly right and lost sight of the twinkle. Something was out there, not on shore; not a producer of light, just a reflector. I moved the light back slightly to the left and it appeared again, blinking on and off between the gusts of snow.

Turning around, I dropped the rope to the snow and placed my foot on it. Ripping the mitt and glove from my left hand, I stashed them inside my snow suit and zipped up the front. Holding the rope in my hand I formed an O with my thumb and forefinger and ran back down the length of rope, snapping it vertically out of the snow. The burning pain of the cold and the rope's stiffness tore at my hand, sending jolts of pain up my elbow that became nearly unbearable as I heard the sled's rough idle over the storm.

As I neared the end of the rope I ever so gently pulled a few feet of slack and placed the flashlight in the snow facing the sled. Stumbling in the dark, I reached the sled by following the sound of the engine. Heading to the front, I found the headlight and kicked with my foot until the right ski hit my boot. Reaching down, I pulled until the snowmobile was facing the same direction as the rope. The bitterness on my left hand forced me to change gloves and bare my right hand as I maneuvered the sled to the flashlight, which I snagged from the snow and paused to place in my pocket. Gently holding the rope in my bare hand, I sat Indian-style on the seat and eased the machine alongside the rope as I carefully traced its path back to the large knot. Within seconds the large knot numbed my hand, and I looked up to see the miraculous glimmer now framed by the headlight. Letting the rope drag behind, I throttled up and suddenly came up to a Christmas tree, propped at a crooked angle in the ice. Pulling my flashlight out, I spun in a circle and identified a few others clearly marking the path home. Again opening the seat I jammed the rope inside, leaving it hooked to the tow bar as I slammed the seat over it, urgent to move on.

Turning to go, I shined the flashlight back to the tree and again caught a glimmer in its dead branches. Stepping to it I reached in and touched a cold, hard object with my frozen right hand. Pulling it toward me I held it to the light and looked with amazement upon the delicate, whitish-blue glass star. This simple symbolic ornament had survived all of this. With newly experienced delicacy I gently tucked it into my upper pocket and returned to the snowmobile.

With a careful eye on the trees I sped to the shore and saw with relief the lights of the village just before I jumped the ice bridge onto land. As I pulled alongside the old warehouse the door cracked open and Constantine stepped into the cold. He eyed me warily, looking from the sled to the rope jutting from the seat to my head missing its helmet. He followed me into the warmth of the building and asked, "Where's your helmet, boy? What happened out there?"

I stood close to the old barrel stove and dropped my stiff, cold gloves on it. Reaching into my upper pocket I pulled out the precious star with great care and caution. Cons stood looking at me as I carefully inspected the star for damage. Finally I raised my head and stared into his eyes, nodding slightly. He raised an eyebrow and smiled, looking hard into my eyes, searching deeply. He nodded knowingly as we stood very close in the warmth of the well-stoked wood stove.